Oliver Prescott Hiller

American National Lyrics, and Sonnets

Oliver Prescott Hiller

American National Lyrics, and Sonnets

ISBN/EAN: 9783744784184

Printed in Europe, USA, Canada, Australia, Japan

Cover: Foto ©Andreas Hilbeck / pixelio.de

More available books at **www.hansebooks.com**

AMERICAN

NATIONAL LYRICS,

AND

SONNETS.

By O. PRESCOTT HILLER,

AUTHOR OF

"THE PLEASURES OF RELIGION, AND OTHER POEMS."

BOSTON:

OTIS CLAPP, 3, BEACON STREET.

NEW YORK: 20, COOPER INSTITUTE.

1860.

TO

MY BELOVED COUNTRY

I VENTURE TO DEDICATE

𝔗𝔥𝔢𝔰𝔢 𝔏𝔶𝔯𝔦𝔠𝔰.

February, 1860.

CONTENTS.

NATIONAL LYRICS.

SONNETS.

NATIONAL LYRICS.

ODE FOR INDEPENDENCE DAY.

Day of a nation's birth !
Let cannon roar, and shake the solid earth :
Let trumpets blow, and to the world proclaim
The high " United " name.
And peal the clanging bells
With music loud that **tells**
A Princess born this glorious day, I **ween**,—
Daughter of Truth the king, and Freedom **queen**.

Amid the battle's storm
Young America[1] was born,
And nursed by warriors' hands :
Her little feeble form
Looked helpless and forlorn,
Begirt by hostile bands.

B

But the mighty God above
Spread wide his shield of love,
    And guarded her from harm ;
And the tiny infant grew—
As Time with swift wings flew—
    Supported by His arm.

And now she stands in might,
A giantess in height,
    Dauntless and strong ;
And loudly doth proclaim
Majestic Freedom's name,
And all the nations wide the cry prolong.

And louder shall it ring,
    Farther and farther sound,
Till trembling tyrants hide beneath the ground.
    Then shall the nations sing,
    And grateful offerings bring
    To the high God, their King ;
And all the world His holy name adore,
And in His smile rejoice for evermore.

BUNKER'S HILL.

Mark ye yon glorious height?
　List while I tell :
'Twas there, in freedom's fight,
Bold yeomen, for the right,
Battled with Britain's might,
　And Warren fell.

At earliest blush of morn,
　Their bands were spied,
Toiling, and somewhat worn,
(But not a look forlorn)
With breastwork to adorn
　The hill's green side.

At once the foemen showered
   Their angry shot :
But not a yeoman cowered,
And not a head was lowered,
While Prescott[2] bravely towered,
   And heeded not.

At length the ranks came on,
   The work to storm :
Alas ! how many a one
Looked last upon the sun,
As to some silent gun
   He spread his form.

Now " Fire !" the Colonel cried—
   " I see their eyes :"[3]
And hundreds fell and died,
As streamed that fire-sheet wide,
And wounded wretches cried
   Up to the skies.

Onward again they came—
   Again they fell
Before that burst of flame :
For deadly was the aim,
Pointed in freedom's name,
   By freemen well.

At last, superior force
   Slowly prevailed :
But many a bleeding corse
Told 'twas a sad resource,
The victors had the worse,—
   Triumph bewailed.

That battle, fought so well
   By freedom's band,
Tolled the oppressors' knell,
And spread a charmèd spell,
That made each bosom swell
   Throughout the land.

Remembering the deeds
  Of that proud day,
Our country in its needs,
When wrapped in mourning weeds,
Held fast the Hope that leads
  To victory.

This monument[4] now rears
  Its lofty head :
Delivered from our fears,
We give our thanks and tears,
While memory endears
  The glorious dead.

And may the noble pile
  Forever stand,
Rousing men's hearts the while,
Throughout the world, to toil
Till freed their native soil
  From tyrant's hand.

Now praised be God, the Lord,
  Who saved our cause ;
And may His mighty Word
Spread truth and peace abroad,
Till in all lands adored
  His name and laws.

TO THE MEMORY OF WASHINGTON.

Thou great of soul, whose noble aim
 To serve thy country, and to bless
 With freedom, peace, and happiness,
  Is highest fame,—
To thee we bow in gratitude
  And reverent love :
May Heaven's most rich beatitude
  Bless thee above !

In days of darkness, when the foe
 Had swept the land, and all seemed lost,—
 When Freedom's barque, long tempest-tossed,
  Was sinking low,—
Thy head was seen amid the gloom,
  Bared to the gale :
Thy eye beheld the impending doom,
  But did not quail.

In the hour of triumph, when the war,
  Bravely maintained and carried through
  To victory, upon thee drew
    All eyes from far,—
Then low in gratitude to Heaven
    Thy thanks were poured,
And back with modesty was given
    Thy country's sword.

Again, reluctant, called to power,
  The nation's good thy only end,
  From thy firm purpose nought could bend,
    In adverse hour :[5]
Conscience thy guide, and God thy stay,
    What couldst thou fear ?
Wisdom herself marked out thy way,
    And Peace stood near.

Vulgar ambition, in thy breast
  No place retained : thy duty done,
  Thou soughtst but that life's setting sun
    Might sink to rest :

How glorious that setting ! calm
    As summer eve,
When golden skies and airs of balm
    Sweet memories leave.

Great Washington ! thy name shall stand
    Through time,—a model to the brave,
    The hope of every struggling slave
        In every land.
Parents to youth thy course shall show,
        Example high :
Millions from thee the way shall know
        To live, to die.

MOUNT VERNON.[6]

Here sleeps the hero !   Lightly, lightly tread !
The place is sacred.   Here the noble dead
Reposes from his toils and triumphs now !
Uncover, friends, and low with reverence bow.

The tomb of Washington !   A lofty soul
Inspired that clay.   But to a higher goal
It winged its soaring flight, and rests in peace
Before the throne of God, where troubles cease.

Yet in this tomb remains the mortal form,
Which that high spirit wore : the battle's storm
This frame hath stood : this hand hath grasped the sword,
When o'er the field the tide of battle poured.

The eye is here, though closed and sightless now,
Which ne'er before proud England's host would bo
From hosts angelic in the courts above,
His looks now meet with answering looks of love.

Hovers his spirit near? and doth it keep
Perpetual watch, in daylight and in sleep,
Over the land that once it loved so well?
Angels of light, that see him—tell, O tell!

Majestically stand these trees around,
And hymn the hero's dirge with solemn sound.
Depart we, friends; this lesson on our heart
Deeply impressed, to go and do *our* part.

THE WASHINGTON MONUMENT.[1]

Ay, pile the marble : let the structure rise,
Till it shall mingle with the blue, bright skies :
That stone's not whiter than his spotless fame :
Those skies not loftier than his deathless name.

In other times, great Pyramids arose,
Proud kings' momentoes, guarding their repose :
The monuments still stand—but lo ! of whom ?
Their dust and name together found a tomb.

But when this obelisk, that now we raise,
About to scatter far and wide its blaze,
Shall fall, and crumble back again to dust—
Shall change and pass away, as all things must,—

Still his great name shall bright and brighter shine,

As rolling ages weave time's lengthening line :

This land shall ne'er forget its noblest son,

The patriot pure, the peerless Washington.

Or should Time's rushing tide sweep all away,

And leave no vestige of this nation's day ;—

Should e'en the globe itself be crushed and riven,

He still will live,—his name is found in heaven.

THE MARTYRS OF THE REVOLUTION.

With bleeding feet the men tramp on, tramp on,
  Their red tracks leaving on the frozen snow :—
" O, is it thus that freedom's prize is won ?"
  Their feeling leader said, with heart of woe.

" Cheer up, my men, cheer up ! march on, march on !
  'Tis for your wives and little ones ye fight :
Ere long a glorious victory will be won,
  And then bright days will follow this dark night."

Their loved commander's stirring voice they heard,
  And quicker stepped along the frozen snow ;
But sad and gloomily, without a word,
  They marched, with lips compressed and looks of woe.

Little the food they'd taken all the day;
　　Thin were they clad against the wintry cold :
And soon upon the road some sinking lay,
　　Their sufferings ended in dark death's stern hold.

Their leader saw : " O God of hosts," he cried,
　　" Whose arm in days of yore the faithful stayed,
Forsake us not ! behold, our hearts are tried !
　　O, in this day of darkness lend thy aid !''

The prayer was heard.   The same Almighty Power,
　　That rescued Israel from Egyptian bands,
Sustained our fathers through that gloomy hour,
　　Strengthened their sinking hearts, upheld their hands.

But ere the end was reached, and freedom gained,
　　How many a noble spirit lay full low !
We reap the blessings by their death attained,—
　　Ours the good, but theirs the wounds and woe.

O shall we not our grateful tributes bring ?
   Their names with reverence speak, their memory love ?
Perchance our thankful hearts and songs will spring,
   And move their spirits in the courts above.

Yet this the truest homage we can pay,—
   To prize the parting gifts they died to gain :
This sacred freedom never to betray,
   This glorious Union ever to maintain.

BRITANNIA RULES THE WAVES NO MORE.

Britannia rules the waves no more :
    Her trident's snapped in twain :
    Over the tossing main
She stalks not now as she was wont before.

Who broke her towering pride ?
    The youthful Giant of the West :
    To do Heaven's high behest
Was he raised up, and with a stride
He struck the ocean-sceptre from her side.

  She had abused the power that God had given :
Proud of her strength, she raged the wide sea o'er,
    And as the oak is riven
    By thunderbolt of heaven,
So roared her cannon round each distant shore,
Rending stout castle walls, and adding store to store.

Weak neutrals she distressed ;
And with tyrannic force
Seizing their ships and goods,—her proud behest
She bade them do, or suffer.   And, in course,
She worried that young Giant of the West :
His seamen she impressed ;
And many hundred natives of his shore
From home and friends with cruel hands she tore. [8]

Up rose he to the fight :
He knew his foeman's might,
But knew he, also, God is with the right.
He thought of former days, when, but a child,
He had withstood the tyrant mother's rod ;
And now again the oppressor should be foiled,
Or he would lay his bones beneath the sod.

*   *   *   *   *   *   *

'Twas on a summer's day.   The Guerriere,
A British frigate, with her sails all set,
Was dashing on.   At her mast-head she bare

A broom,[9] to sweep the seas of all she met :—
        The boast was not tried yet.

" Ho there ! a sail upon the weather-bow !"
All hearts rejoice.   " Ay ! helmsman, bear up now."
" She comes, she comes : a frigate."—" Ha ! that's well !
What is her nation ?   French or Yankee ? tell !
O, 'tis American—the stripes and stars !
Hurrah for England !   By the glorious Mars
A noble prize she'll make for our fine tars."

" She nears, she nears.   Give her a broadside now :—
    The shot told well : now watch her smoke there, men.
What ? no return ? they are asleep there !—How ?
    No firing yet ?   Give her another, then :
    Another—and another—and again.
O shame ! for shame ! to strike without a blow !"—
    O never fear : she'll wake up by and by :
She's taking her position : soon she'll show.
    Look there ! her flag is flying free and high :
    There's no strike there : it says, " *to do or die.*"

"There gleam the flashes, sure enough, at last."
In pours the shot—and thick, and hot, and fast—
    Faster and faster, and on every side
    Showers the iron tempest wide :
    From stem to stern—above—below—
    Through ports, through bulwarks, crashing go
    Round shot, chain shot, bar shot, all
    The iron monsters that the soul appal.
Red flows the blood : down go the wounded men :
Up rise the shrieks and groans :—again—again :—
    There is no ceasing, no suspense
Of crashings dire—no hiding, no defence ;
On every hand the dreadful splinters fly—
    Extinguished 's many a flashing eye :
Arms, legs, and backs are broken by the shot—
The iron storm pours on and heeds them not.
The decks are slippery :—bodies lie about
    From which the living soul 's gone out :
The decks are slippery, slippery with gore :—
O horrors ! this is war—this, this is war !
There goes the mizen-mast o'er the vessel's side
    Into the smoking tide :

The foremast totters, too,—and now the main :—
Down, down they go—they're broken full in twain.
" Strike, strike the flag," the captain loudly cries :
" 'Tis hard, but there's no help :—a log she lies."

Sudden the thunders cease : the crashing tempests lull.
She nears.   " What ship is that ?"—" The Constitution,—
      Hull."
" Well, there's my sword," said Dacres : " hard for me ;
But here I lie : I've done my best, you see."

" Fortune of war, sir," Hull politely said.
" Now, Mr. Morris,* overboard the dead—
Up with their wounded—pass the prisoners here :
She's cut to pieces—quite beyond repair :
Must blow her up : they took her from the French,
And we from them : now give her a sea trench."

So the first conflict ends ; and Britain's might
Of name and fame is bowed.[10] God save the right !

---

* The late Commodore Morris, then first lieutenant of the *Constitution*.

KENTUCKY THE BRAVE.

(*A Western Wood-Song.*)

" Kentucky the Brave " 's my song,
" Kentucky the Brave " prolong :
   She stands on her feet,
   And there's none can beat
     Kentucky.

In the olden time, the bear
Roamed through the forest here ;
And he climbed the honey tree,
And robbed the hope of the bee.
But sudden the hunter came,
And his rifle's crack and flame
Through the forest rang and flashed,
And luckless Bruin dashed
   To the ground
   With a wound.

Chorus.—Hurrah ! " Kentuck " 's my song,

    " Kentucky the Brave," prolong :

    She stands on her feet,

    And there's none can beat

        Kentucky.

    At length the country's call

    Was heard,—" To the Southern wall !"

    For the British foe had come

    From their distant island home,

    To take our noble city,

    Its " beauty " and its " booty."

    From France and Spain they'd come,

    These men of fife and drum,

    For Bonaparte they'd beat,

    And forced him to retreat.

Chorus.—Hurrah ! " Kentuck " 's my song, &c.

    And shall these fellows tear

    Our lovely maidens' hair ?

    Shall they burn New Orleans down,

    As they did fair Washington ?   .

Kentucky answered " *No!*"

And aimed her rifles low

At the breasts of the coming foe.

And down—and down—they fell

In heaps, in their ranks, pell-mell ;

And away the living run,

And the battle's fought and won.[11]

Chorus.—Hurrah ! " Kentuck " 's my song, &c.

BUENA VISTA.

Buena Vista sleeps :
Along its moonlit steeps
  The midnight breezes blow :
While o'er the lighted plain
The ghosts of warrior men
  Are gliding to and fro.

And when the morning breaks,
Still silent Nature wakes
  O'er the deserted ground :
The eagle screams above,
While greedy vultures move,
  Heavy, from mound to mound.

Not always, o'er yon hill,
The sun rose clear and still,
  As we behold to-day;
But clanging trumpets woke
Armies to battle's shock,
  And smoke obscured the sky.

Proud Santa Anna came,
With twice ten thousand men,
  To take brave Taylor's band :
" Yield you," he fiercely said,
" Or soon, among the dead,
  Your troops shall strew the land."

Calmly the hero stood,
And viewed the approaching flood :
  " I cannot yield, you see,
For here I'm placed to fight :
We'll make (if you've the might)
  A new Thermopylae."[12]

Bold Illinois was there,
And Indiana's share,
    And Mississippi, three :
And Arkansaw's array,
And, led by valiant Clay,
    Kentucky's chivalry.

No hireling bands were these,
Wherewith proud despots tease
    Alike their friends and foes ;
But daring volunteers,
America's brave peers—
    No other peers she knows.

'Twas Washington's birth-day :
And should we feel dismay
    At yon advancing host ?
" No ! no ! the Hero's eye
Beams on us from the sky—
    The battle can't be lost."

From morn till evening hour,
The battle raged with power
  O'er hill and dale and plain :
Ah ! many a spirit bold
His last camp-tale has told,
  Now pale among the slain.

Brave Clay is gone—and Yell,
Hardin, M'Kee just fell :—
  On, still, their masses pour :
Backward they're driven there,
But crowds are coming here :—
  Stand firm, or all is o'er.

" Bring up your batteries,"
Old Rough-and-Ready* cries,—
  " Your grape, Bragg,†—quick—more grape "'
The faltering column breaks,
Then soon to flight betakes :
  We breathe—a near escape.

---

* A *soubriquet* of Gen. Taylor's.   † Capt. Bragg, of the Artillery.

We bivouacked on the field,

Expecting day would yield

   New conflicts with their powers :

We woke—the foe had fled,

Leaving his heaps of dead :—

   Buena Vista's ours.[13]

AMERICA'S TRUE GLORY.

Seek not, my Country, that ignoble fame,
　Which springs from conquest of a brother's soil:
Do fraud and violence yield a lofty name?
　Is't Great to snatch the fruits of others' toil?

Away! away! speak not of " Destiny:"[14]
　There is no destiny nor fate but God:
His law is justice, his rule liberty,
　His plan—to all the largest, highest good.

Be sure He will the humblest right defend,
　And cast the base oppressor headlong down:
Wrong triumphs for a time,—but, in the end,
　Pain follows sin, as sure as night the sun.[15]

Has Providence not given a noble land,
   Spreading from sea to sea ? what need we more ?
And shall we now provoke His mighty hand,
   By robbing others of their little store ?

O no ! but be it ours to show the world
   The high example of a nation's truth :
Upon our Country's flag, where'er unfurled,
   This motto write, held from our Country's youth :—

" No wrong to suffer, and no wrong to do !"
   Reading these words, the strong shall stand in awe,
And weaker nations may their course pursue,
   Fearing no harm, while keeping right and law.

The glory of America shall be,
   To see her people happy, wise, and true :
All avenues to good thrown open free,
   All rights supported, to each man his due ;

For all, fair Learning's table amply spread,—
 The noblest feast, the banquet of the mind :
Freedom secured, for which our fathers bled ;
 Religion's blessings to no sect confined.

Thus shall our Country prove a glorious land,
 To all the world a shining light afar :
The Lord will grant us His protecting hand,
 And all shall hail the beaming Western Star.

ON THE DEATH OF WEBSTER.[16]

The statesman has gone to his last, long home,
 Bewailed by a nation's tears:
His cold form has now passed to the silent tomb,
 His spirit to other spheres.

America's hope and pride is low:
 She mourns for her patriot son.
No sectional feeling or thought did he know,
 His country to him was ONE.[17]

The East and the West, the North and the South,
 Were but parts of one glorious land:
He pleaded for all with eloquent mouth,
 And laboured with earnest hand.

The Union was ever his foremost aim ;
    For that he would live or die :
He has gone :—may his country's " United " name
    Endure, as he hoped, for aye !

" I live," were his dying words, " I still live :"
    'Tis true, illustrious one !
Thou liv'st in the fame that a world can give,
    Thou liv'st in thy duty done ;

Thou liv'st in thy country's love and pride,
    In memory's tributes given :
Thou liv'st in a better land beside,
    Thou livest, we trust, in heaven.

    November, 1852.

MY COUNTRY.

America, my country, far away
  I sojourn here upon a foreign shore ;
Yet oft to thee I turn, by night, by day,
  And long to look upon thy face once more.

When low the sun is sinking in the West,
  I stand and gaze upon his going down,
And wish that I, like him, might sink to rest
  Near that dear distant land I call my own.

When 'twilight lingers' in the evening sky,
  And through its veil looks forth the Western Star,
O then I fancy 'tis the spirit-eye
  Of my own Home, thus beaming from afar.

When Night hath kindled up her stellar fires,
   And silence wide broods o'er the sleeping earth,—
Then oft, in dreams, the soul (which never tires)
   Sweetly presents the country of my birth.

Dear native land! by absence made more dear,
   Nor always from thee shall I distant stray:
My duty done, how will I hasten near,
   Upon thy lap my weary head to lay!

SCOTLAND, 1852.

SONNETS.[1]

I.

FRANKLIN.

Sage of America! thy country's pride!
  In early days, ere yet our youthful land
  Had won a nation's name, thy daring hand
Mastered the lightning—drew it to thy side.

Soon did the wondrous news spread far and wide ;
  And Europe's lofty, scientific band
  Paid homage to the man, whose magic wand
Could rule the elements, and stay their tide.

Nor Science, only, thine, but wisdom too ;
Wisdom in senates and in courts, that knew
  Man's heart, as well as Nature's,—could control
    With simple words the lightning flash of thought ;
    And, more than all, the wisdom pure that taught
To curb the fiery passions of the soul.

II.

JAMES OTIS AND PATRICK HENRY.

Twin patriot orators ! Your tongues of fire
First roused our people to resistance stern
'Gainst British tyranny; and hearts did burn,
At your appeal, with freemen's noble ire.

As, in the olden time, the stirring lyre
And Demosthenic voice the Greeks did turn
Against proud Philip,—so did ye inspire
Your country's heart king George's yoke to spurn.

Virginia's fire and Massachusett's truth
Went hand in hand,—stern North and glowing South
What could withstand their brave, united might ?
So, ever, side by side, in danger's hour,
In council or the field, their mingled power
Shall raise our land to glory's loftiest height.

III.

INDEPENDENCE HALL, PHILADELPHIA.

Around—the great departed seem to stand,
    As in the days of yore, with solemn mien ;
    And, stepping forward, on the table lean,
And calmly, one by one, affix their hand

To the great document that freed our land :
    Methinks I now behold the lofty scene,
    And hear the moving pen, in the serene
Yet earnest stillness of that patriot band.

Bold Jefferson is there, and Adams, too,
Franklin the wise, and Hancock brave and true :
    A nobler council never met in hall.
Methinks their spirits hover round us still,
And bid us their high purposes fulfil,
    Nor ever let this glorious Union fall.

IV.

FANEUIL HALL, BOSTON.

Old Faneuil !   Oft, how oft these walls have rung
  With freemen's voices !   In Colonial days,
  The orator here kindled freedom's blaze
With magic words, as if a syren sung.

Here Otis flamed; here Quincy bravely flung
  His wise words forth, men's hearts and hopes to raise
  Here Adams stood before his country's gaze :
On Webster's accents, here, what crowds have hung !

Cradle of freedom ! on these walls I read
  The scroll of patriot names that ne'er shall die :
America's Walhalla ![(2) here the seed
  Of lofty thoughts is sown, and virtues high ;
    And oft the tears of memory here shall fall,
    As future freemen tread this sacred hall.

V.

BOSTON COMMON.

ause here and look around.   This ancient tree,[3]
   'Neath which we stand, strange sights of yore hath seen.
   List to its whispering boughs—which still are green—
hat chronicles it tells to thee and me :

   In my young days, here roamed the savage free,
   And drank of yonder crescent pond, I ween;
   But strangers stood where natives once had been,—
he white man's face these ancient woods did see.

' At length the red-coats came.   Along the plain
   Their burnished muskets glittered in the sun,
   And white tents gleamed.   But soon their day was done,
And never here their feet shall tread again."
   Well done, my stout old elm ! and thou shalt stand,
   To grace, for many a year, this beauteous land.

VI.

BATTLE MONUMENT, BALTIMORE.

Glory to those who bravely fought and fell
   In Baltimore's defence ! their names read here.
Let fathers, as they pass, their children tell
   Ever to hold the martyrs' memory dear :

And, as they listen, their young breasts shall swell
   With patriotic fire; and, spurning fear,
They will resolve—should ever foes come near—
   To die, if need be, for their country's weal.

Hither came valiant Ross, but ne'er returned :—
He, who our stately Capitol had burned
   With Vandal hand; but here his fate he met.
May all invaders of this nation's soil
A like fate find, and rue their hopeless toil !
   " God and our country !" be our motto yet !

VII.

PLYMOUTH ROCK.

The Rock of Plymouth—freedom's far-famed stone !
  O long **this rock** had waited for its day,
  While slow the rolling ages **passed away**.
At length **a** sail appeared, far off and lone,

Feeling its way across the shoals unknown.
  Nearer it came, and now the Mayflower lay,
  Anchored secure within the sheltering bay ;
And Pilgrims' careworn faces hopeful shone.

They landed here, beneath the lofty sky,
  Upon this stepping-stone which God **had laid**,
And soon began a structure broad and **high**,
  At **once** for Freedom and Religion made.
    By **these** two powers upheld, our State **shall stand**
    Through circling years, a good and glorious **land**.

VIII.

THE DANISH TOWER AT NEWPORT.[4]

Canst thou not speak, and tell what thou hast seen?
    Wilt thou in solemn silence ever stand,
    And gloom abroad upon this wondering land,
Spreading mysterious awe?   What hast thou been?

Who set thee here? what do these columns mean?
    Art thou the work of that brave Northman band,
    Who crossed the wave, and stood upon this strand,
Ages before Columbus' bold marine?

Yes! they would mark the exploit they achieved,
    And raised this monument to tell the tale:
New sounds the forest solitudes perceived,
    The clink of chisel, and the clank of mail.
        But soon the strangers perished in the wood,
        Or else, returning, sank beneath the flood.

IX.

LEDYARD, THE TRAVELER.[5]

One of our early heroes ! born to roam,
  The trackless wilds of nature to explore :
  Roving o'er sea and land, from shore to shore,
In the wide world he found his best-loved home.

Forsaking college halls and learned tome,
  He launches forth with rough-hewn boat and oar :
Down the Connecticut behold him come,
  Heedless of perilous falls or rapids' roar.

A sailor's life and then a soldier's tries.
  With the bold Cook he sails the world around :
Through Lapland's snows, 'neath bleak Siberia's skies,
  He seeks, a-foot, to reach Earth's farthest bound :
    Then turns the secret of the Nile to find,—
    But Death to grander secrets called his mind.

E

X.

ROBERT FULTON.

Our noble Fulton! lofty honors pay
　To him who bravely labors for his kind,
　Whose conquests are the triumphs of the mind,
Who opens to the world a brighter day.

Fast by swift Hudson's bank a vessel lay :
　No sail has she to woo the fickle wind ;
　Yet see! she moves :—sure, Genii push behind,
So bravely up the stream she makes her way.

Yes! 'tis bold Fulton's genius urging there,
　And Fire and Water work at his command :
Stronger are these than e'en the Powers of air,
　To waft the stately ship from land to land.
　　And now the world reaps freely of his toil :
　　Honor to Fulton and his native soil ! [6]

XI.

WASHINGTON ALLSTON.

Upon our walls, thy genius, Allston, beams
  From charming landscape and historic scene :
  Italia's bowers, and plains, and skies serene,
Here glow in beauty, like a land of dreams.

Thy pencil, too, hath traced still loftier themes
  The dead reviving at a touch, is seen : [7]
  And mark profane Belshazzar's frighted mien,
As on the wall mysterious writing gleams.

But, Allston, thou to higher worlds hast soared :
  More beauteous landscapes shine before thy view,
Sublimer scenes are all around thee poured,
  Than e'er on earth thine eye or fancy knew.
    He who, in love, thy lofty powers hath given,
    Now bids thee paint the scenery of heaven.

XII.

TO WASHINGTON IRVING.

The father of our literature ! to thee
  Our Country owes its place in glory's line :
  The glory, not of arms—more pure and fine,
The fame of genius, letters, poesy.

How oft, in youth, thy book upon my knee,
  I've sat and dreamed, and wished the power were mine,
To clothe in words of rhythmic melody
  Delightful thoughts, sweet fancies, such as thine.

I thank thee, Irving, for those pleasant hours;
  And if, in riper years, my task has been
To write on graver themes, perchance some flowers
  Culled from thy stem may here and there be seen.
    Yet seek I not to rival thee, but own
    That in thy charming sphere thou reign'st alone.

XIII.

TO POWERS, THE SCULPTOR.

Bright forms in thy fine fancy, Powers, arise,
    And soon in clay they stand exposed to view :
    At length they shine in marble's brilliant hue,
And beam all living to our wondering eyes :—

The "Greek Slave," shown in nature's bashful guise ;
    Fair " Eve," about to taste, but soon to rue ;
    Lofty "America," with freedom true,
Though trampling crowns, still pointing to the skies.

Toil on, great sculptor! still bring forth to light
New shapes that gleam before thy mental sight,
    And fix them in the firm, enduring stone.
So shall thy country in her son delight ;
    So shall thy works to future times be known,
    And charm the world when upward thou art gone.

XIV.

LIEUT. LYNCH'S EXPLORATION OF THE DEAD SEA.

Here lie the buried cities of the plain.
    The heavy waters sleep in death's repose:
    No living thing this desolation knows:
An awful silence round the shores doth reign.

Three thousand years these waters thus have lain,—
    When lo! a stranger comes! where Jordan flows,
    His rushing billows issuing amain,—
Comes the bold man: an iron boat he rows.

And now he wakes these waters with the oar—
A touch and splash they ne'er have felt before—
    And wends his way across the sluggish deep.
Into its silent depths he drops his lead,
Explores their oozy, chrystal-covered bed,
    And leaves his Country's flag to fan their sleep.[8]

XV.

DR. KANE'S DISCOVERY OF THE POLAR SEA.

Laurels for thee and for thy Country, Kane!
　　Through icy barriers thou hadst made thy way,
　　In search of England's lost ones;[9] day by day,
Scanning the frozen wilderness in vain.

But lo! where cold Charles drives his starry wain
　　Forever round the pole,—where not a ray
　　Of Sol's all cheering light for months doth play,
But Winter spreads around his drear domain,—

Behold an open sea! How sweet to view
　　The free waves dancing in the polar wind,
Their icy fetters gone! Now launch anew
　　Thy bold bark, Kane, and the deep secret find.
　　　　Ah no! exhausted nature calls thee home,
　　　　No more, no more, those northern wilds to roam.[10]

XVI.

THE ATLANTIC TELEGRAPH.

Wonder of wonders! see! an ocean chain
    Binding the distant nations into one !
The boast of Xerxes now no more is vain :
    The task of fettering the sea is done.

The spirit-world draws nearer.   As the Sun
    Of Righteousness disperses sin and pain,—
    As faith and love are joined and no more twain,—
So triumphs over space and time are won.

A FRANKLIN drew the lightning from the skies,—
    A MORSE had harnessed it to learning's car.
Across the continents he drove his prize,
    Conveying messages of peace and war;
        And now, like Neptune, gallops through the seas,
        Outstripping far the steamship and the breeze.

XVII.

THE FATHER OF WATERS.[11]

In by-gone times, great River, thou didst pour
   Thy swelling flood through solitudes profound,
   When from thy silent bosom came no sound
Of Indian paddle or of white man's oar.

Perchance, long ages ere on Egypt's shore
   The slave-built pyramids a place had found,
   Here, on thy borders, stood the grass-grown mound,
Raised by a race unknown, long since no more.

At length the wandering red man found his way
   To these green banks, and chose them for his home,
And war-whoops woke the echoes.   But the day
   Of white men's power arrived; and now the foam
     Of thousand rushing steamers whites thy wave,
     And cities rise above the red man's grave.

XVIII.

THE BOSTON LATIN SCHOOL.

Schola Latina, to my memory dear,
  Methinks I hear again thy matin bell
  (The sound that every laggard knew full well)
Toll o'er the waters to my listening ear.

Methinks those school-day scenes once more appear:
  I hear the anxious youths reciting tell
  How proud Rome triumphed, and how Carthage fell
Æneas' exploits, and poor Dido's tear.

Boston's chief glory, education meet
  For all her children, howe'er poor or low,
Hath this its crown, that who with ready feet
  Would mount the steeps of science, or would go
    Along the silver streams of classic lore,
    May find a way prepared, an open door.

Scotland, 1852.

XIX.

HARVARD COLLEGE.

Harvard, thy classic walls before my view
  In memory rise.   Teacher of ancient lore,
   Nurse of our fathers' minds in days of yore,
America's first Alma Mater true.

In Massachusetts'* walls,—when soft the dew
  On moonlit groves[12] was falling, off I tore
   My eyes from classic page away, to pore
Over the sweet still lines the moonbeams drew.

The air seemed haunted : stately forms of Rome,
  With lofty Grecian sages, glided by ;
And, in the midst, bright Shakspeare's face would come,
  And sightless Milton, in his majesty :
    While, from the throng, tall laureled Fame would wave,
    And bid me join that band beyond the grave.

* The name of one of the College halls.

XX.

TO THE RIVER OHIO.

My beautiful Ohio! how I love
  Thy winding stream! thy pretty wooded isles,
  Thy verdant banks, whereon the blue sky smiles,
And ever beams the golden sun above.

How oft, at evening, do I silent rove
  By thy sweet side,—as meditation whiles
  Away the pensive hours, when all the toils
Of garish day are o'er, and feelings move.

On the opposing shore, gleam one by one
  The evening lamps of many peaceful homes:
In the dusk graveyard there, life's task now done,
  Many repose beneath the dewy tombs,—
    Their souls, I trust, in heaven. When comes my hour,
    Thither draw me, too, Saviour, by thy power.

NOTES.

NOTES TO THE NATIONAL LYRICS.

[1] Page 1. *Young America.*

The name "America,"—though, geographically, it signifies the whole continent,—yet, politically, is often applied to the United States.

[2] Page 4. *While Prescott bravely towered.*

The commander at the redoubt was Colonel William Prescott (General Warren had not yet taken a command, and was only a volunteer). Col. Prescott had already seen service in the "old French war." His figure was tall and commanding, and, as he walked back and forth on the redoubt, cheering his men at their work, and setting them an example of fearlessness, he presented a striking object. Gen. Gage, who was reconnoitering with his glass from Copp's Hill, inquired of Counselor Willard by his side, "Who is that officer commanding?" Willard recognized Colonel Prescott (who was his brother-in-law). "Will he fight?" asked Gage. "Yes, sir, depend upon it," was the reply, "to the last drop of his blood; but I cannot answer for his men."

[3] Page 4. *I see their eyes.*

The men had been commanded not to fire till the enemy came so near that they "could see the whites of their eyes." "When the space," says an account, "between the assailants and the redoubt was narrowed to the appointed span, the word was spoken, and the deadly flashes burst forth. The slaughter was awful: out of an attacking force of 4000, the killed and wounded numbered 1054. Among these, the officers were particularly numerous, as the marksmen had orders 'to aim at the handsome coats.' The green grass was crimsoned with the life blood of hundreds. The front rank of the British was nearly obliterated. As the wind rolled away the smoke, some of the wounded were seen crawling with the last energies of life from the gory heaps of the dying and the dead. The cries of the sufferers, groans and prayers, impious oaths, and fond invocations of absent loved ones, were all strangely mingled with the shouts of victory that rang from the redoubt. Twice were the British fairly and completely driven from the hill."

[4] Page 6. *This monument now rears*
Its lofty head.

The monument is a granite obelisk, 220 feet in height, and is probably the finest structure of the kind in the world. The corner-stone was laid on the 17th of June, 1825, the fiftieth anniversary of the battle, and the cap-stone was placed, July 23, 1842,—the erection having occupied, with intervals, a period of seventeen years.

[5] Page 9. *In adverse hour.*

The course of Washington, while President, in firmly with-standing the tide of popular feeling, while doing what he believed to be his duty and for the best good of the country, in the matter of the " British Treaty," in 1794,—displayed true greatness, and afforded one more proof of his utter superiority to any thought of self. He thereby showed, that as popular favor and admiration, in former times, could not entice him from the path of duty, so neither, now, could popular opposition and violence drive him from it : neither sun nor storm could move him.

[6] Page 11. *Mount Vernon.*

The effort now making by the "Ladies' Mount Vernon Association" to secure this sacred spot to the country, is worthy of all praise and of hearty coöperation. Let it be preserved as the nation's shrine,—the Mecca, whither every young American shall feel it a duty, once in his life, to make a pilgrimage.

[7] Page 13. *The Washington Monument.*

The monument, now in process of erection at the National Capital, is to be a grand obelisk, 500 feet in height,— of white marble. In one respect, it will be a great curio-sity : the interior will be incrusted with ornamental stones, bearing devices and inscriptions in honor of Washington : these stones have been sent from all parts of the world,— Sweden, Switzerland, Greece, Italy, and even from Asia and

Africa,—testifying, in a most remarkable manner, to the world-wide admiration and reverence felt for our great countryman.

[8] Page 19.   *And many hundred natives of his shore,*
                From home and friends with cruel hands she tore.

" It has been satisfactorily ascertained," says Cooper, " that the number of impressed Americans on board British ships of war, between the years 1802 and 1812, was seldom less than the entire number of seamen in the American Navy. At the declaration of war, in 1812, the number turned over to the prison-ships for refusing to fight against their country, is said to have exceeded 2000."—*History of the United States' Navy,* vol. ii., chap. 8.

[9] Page 20.   *At her mast-head she bare*
                A broom, to sweep the seas of all she met.

It is said that some of the British commanders, in their arrogance,—like the Dutch admirals of former days,—carried a broom at the mast-head, to signify their ability and intention to sweep all enemies from the seas.

[10] Page 22.   —— *And Britain's might*
                Of name and fame is bowed.

When, in 1812, the United States declared war against Great Britain, they had but the commencement of a navy : they did not yet possess a single ship of the line, and had but seven frigates and a few smaller vessels. Yet with this little force they launched boldly forth on the ocean, to meet the greatest of naval Powers, possessing at that time upwards of 600 vessels of war. The result is known to the world: the fame of British naval invincibility was destroyed forever.

Still, however, we occasionally hear British writers, though in a greatly subdued tone, speak of England as " mistress of the seas." But in what, let it be asked, does the dominion of the seas consist? Does it consist merely in the possession of a great number of ships of war? That is a matter merely of choice: any nation that possesses means and constructive skill can build ships to an indefinite extent. At this moment it is estimated that France has more ships of war than England ;* but does any one suppose that France is mistress of the seas? The question is, are there seamen to man and fight the ships after they are built? That is the true question. And that will depend on two things—first, the extent of the mercantile marine, and secondly, on the aptness of a people for the sea ;— in a word, whether they are what is called a maritime nation. Now, the fact is, that, at the present moment, the maritime resources of the United States are as great and even greater than those of Great Britain, and every year is increasing the difference. In 1855 (we have no later statistics at hand), the mercantile tonnage of the United States was 5,661,416, in 40,500 vessels, while that of Great Britain was but 5,043,270,

* In 1856, France had 547 ships to England's 537.

in 35,960 vessels; and the tonnage of France was only 716,130. Thus it will be seen that the United States now stands first in point of ability to man a navy.

As to the number of ships, has not the United States abundant means in her treasury for building ships of war? has she not the skill to construct them? and she has proved her ability to fight them. If, then, she does not keep afloat an immense navy, it is simply because she does not *choose* to do so: it is not her policy to build vast numbers of ships to rot. Conscious of her own strength and resources, she prefers to maintain only the nucleus of a navy, trusting to her own energies for its quick expansion when an emergency shall call for it.

No! the day of England's dominion of the sea is over. Nor is it to be desired that either the United States or any other nation should usurp it in her place: it is better, both for themselves and for the peace of the world, that there should be two or more great Powers nearly on a par in this respect. And furthermore, it is to be hoped that the period of naval wars is at an end; and that the peaceful ocean, intended by the Creator to be the great highway of nations, over which may be exchanged in security the necessaries and comforts of life, will be no more disturbed by warring navies.

[11] Page 25.   *And the battle's fought and won.*

The battle of New Orleans was one of the most disastrous to the British in which they were ever engaged. It was "Bunker's

Hill" repeated, under still more distressing circumstances : they lost officers, men, fame, everything, without gathering, as at Bunker's Hill, the barren laurel of even a nominal victory. And justly was it so disastrous, for they were now invading a country which they had already injured by years of wrong. Sir Edward Packenham, the commander-in-chief, brother-in-law to the Duke of Wellington,—together with Generals Gibbs and Keane, and 2100 men, were left killed or wounded on the field of battle, and 500 were taken prisoners; while the Americans, shielded by their breastwork of cotton bags, lost but 13 killed and 39 wounded. The battle was fought on the 8th January, 1815, and concluded the war; and it is to be hoped that it will be the last battle ever fought between the kindred nations of England and America.

[12] Page 27. *Thermopylæ.*

The famed pass where Leonidas and his three hundred Spartans kept at bay the whole force of the Persian army, till they were cut to pieces.

[13] Page 30. *Buena Vista's ours.*

The battle of Buena Vista was fought on the 22d and 23d February, 1847. The Mexican army came in sight on the morning of the 22d (Washington's birth-day), and at 11 o'clock on that day sent a summons to General Taylor to surrender his small force;—which was answered by Taylor in the spirit and almost in the words of the Spartan commander, "Come and take them." There was some skirmishing in the latter part of that day, but the main battle was fought on the 23d. The peculiarities of this combat, and the glory of the victory, arose chiefly from the circumstance of the immense disparity between the numbers of the opposing armies,—General Taylor's force consisting of but 5000 men, all volunteers (with the exception of 450 regulars), while Santa Anna had with him 20,000 men, the flower of the Mexican army. The struggle against such odds was necessarily long, obstinate, and bloody ; but, at last, American skill and bravery triumphed.

¹⁴ Page 31.   *Away! away! speak not of* " *Destiny.*"

" We must grow," says the *New York Herald*, " and the Union must extend. We shall, in due process of time, absorb all of Mexico, Central America, Cuba, St. Domingo, Porto Rico, and all the other islands of the Caribbean Sea. European resistance to this *manifest destiny* is continually decreasing." Such is the language of the *New York Herald* of October 13, 1858. We have reason to be thankful that the editor of that reckless journal is not an American, but a foreigner—I am sorry to say, a Scotchman. However long he may have resided on our shores, he seems to have imbibed little of the spirit of religion and morality which actuated the Puritan founders of our country, and which, it is to be hoped, still influences, in a great degree, their descendants. He has brought with him from the

Old World the selfish maxims that have for ages governed the policy of Europe, and which we should shake off from us as we would shake the dust from our feet. Let, rather, the policy inaugurated by the great Washington be our guide. In his " Farewell Address " he has laid down the true principle of our national action, founded on the teachings of the Christian religion,—" to do unto others as we would have men do to us." This, and no other, should be the rule of American policy. Let our policy be principle : let our policy be justice : let our policy be *the right:* this is the only manly, the only noble, the only Christian policy. Leave cunning and chicanery to the states of the Old World, if they will still cling to it : we will meet it with the straightforward *right*, and there is no fear for the result.

We are not to do evil that good may come. If Divine Providence (for there is no such blind goddess as " Destiny ") sees it to be for their own good, and for the good of the world, that Cuba, or Mexico, or other neighboring territories should be brought within the limits of the American Union, the way will be opened to effect the object in a just, legitimate, and honorable manner. But it is a thing we should not anxiously seek after, nor think about: we have territory enough and to spare. Let us be thankful for the blessings we have, and leave others to the enjoyment of theirs.

It should be a source of just pride to Americans that, as yet, the United States have not gained one foot of territory by conquest. To this fact, the case of the acquisition of Texas is no exception,—though by many, ignorant of the circumstances, it is supposed to be so. The Texans valorously fought for their independence against the Mexican tyrant, Santa Anna, and in hard-won battles secured it; and that independence was acknowledged by France and England, as well as by the United States. As an independent nation, she then proposed to unite her destinies to those of the United States, and the application, after being once declined, was at length acceded to. In this there was no just cause of complaint, no violation of the law of nations. Mexico, however, in her Spanish pride and obstinacy, declared that she should regard this step as a cause of war, and blindly attacked us. We repulsed her, and pursued her to her own doors, offering peace at every step: but this she obstinately refused, till she was entirely conquered and lay at our mercy: we had possession of the capital and the whole country. What followed? Did we keep possession, as probably Britain or any other of the European nations would have done? No! we voluntarily gave it up, retaining by treaty only California, for which we paid 12,000,000 of dollars. So honorable a national course, under similar circumstances, is scarcely to be found on the pages of history: England or France can show no such instance of preferring right to might. The upright course of our government also, in preventing, as far as it was possible, the invasion of Cuba and Central America by lawless bands of our own citizens, is a source of just self-gratulation. Let a similar course of national integrity continue to be pursued by the United States in its dealings with other ations, and Americans will have more reason to be proud of their country than if she were mistress of the world.

[15] Page 31. *Pain follows sin, as sure as night the sun.*

National suffering will follow national sin, as surely as with individuals punishment attends wrong-doing. Witness, for instance, the sufferings which the British people have endured, collectively and individually, from the late terrible rebellion in India,—a direct consequence of the unrighteous annexation of Oude: thousands of families, from the lowest to the highest, have been thrown into mourning by it. Note, too, the disastrous effect of her long course of needless and unjust war and conquest, during the forty years preceding the peace of 1815. In addition to the loss of tens of thousands of valuable lives, the nation has been saddled with a debt, the pressure of which is felt, in a greater or less degree, by every family in the country, and will continue to be felt, perhaps, for ages to come. See France, too, with her general poverty and diminished population—the effect of similar wars of conquest. See, also, the severe and lasting punishment inflicted on Russia, for her wicked attempt to seize upon the dominions of Turkey, in 1854:— France and England combined against her, her armies destroyed, her military reputation humbled by defeat after defeat, her Black Sea fleet sunk, her southern capital demolished, and, to conclude the tragedy, the death of her emperor himself,—the result, doubtless, of disappointed ambition. In a good cause, I say

" America against the world !" in a righteous cause we need not fear any Power, nor all the Powers combined : the heart of the great American people would burst forth in a flame which would consume everything before it : a million of men would rush to our standards, and a thousand ships, if need be, would soon float upon the seas. But, in a bad cause, we should be miserably weak. That we were successful in both our wars against England, is not to be ascribed to our own prowess alone, but it was because we were in the right, and Divine Providence fought for us. Glory ! the true glory of a nation is to behold all its citizens dwelling in peace, plenty, knowledge, and righteousness : brave, indeed, in the defence of their homes and just rights,— but never attacking, injuring, or wronging any. The only real glory, individual or national, is the glory of wisdom and good-ness. It is time that the old barbarous notion of glory, the glory of mere *animal courage* and *physical force*,—a notion handed down from the heathen days of Achilles and Alexander —were banished from the Christian world.

[16] Page 34. *On the Death of Webster.*

Daniel Webster, the great statesman, jurist, orator, and patriot, died, at his estate of Marshfield, Massachusetts, Octo-ber 24, 1852. The death of no public man, probably, since that of Washington, ever excited so profound a sensation as did this, throughout the length and breadth of the land.

[17] Page 34.   *No sectional feeling or thought did he know,*
His country to him was ONE.

"When I shall be found, sir," said Mr. Webster in his great speech, in reply to Mr. Hayne, of South Carolina,—"When I shall be found, sir, in my place here in the Senate, or elsewhere, to sneer at public merit, because it happens to spring up beyond the little limits of my own State or neighborhood,—when I shall refuse, for such cause, or for any cause, the homage due to American talent, to elevated patriotism, to sincere devotion to liberty and the country,—or if I see an uncommon endowment of heaven, any extraordinary capacity or virtue in any son of the South,—and if, moved by party prejudice, or gangrened by State jealousy, I get up here to abate a tithe of a hair from his just character or just fame,—may my tongue cleave to the roof of my mouth."

NOTES TO THE SONNETS.

¹ Page 39.   *Sonnets.*

The Sonnet is a very ancient species of poetical composition, dating back as far as the thirteenth century,—the age of the Provençals.   It properly consists of fourteen iambic verses, of eleven syllables (in English, ten), and is divided into two chief parts: the first consists of two divisions, each of four lines (*quadrain*) ; the second of two divisions of three lines (*terzina*). The quadrains have two rhymes, each of which is repeated four times, and, according to the Italian usage, either so that the first, fourth, fifth, and eighth verses rhyme, and, again, the verses between them, the second, third, sixth, seventh ; or, which is rarer, the rhymes alternate ; or, what is still rarer, the first quadrain is written in the first way, and the second in the second.   In the two terzines, there are either three rhymes, each twice repeated, or two rhymes thrice repeated, in all positions.*

Italian sonnets, as seen in Petrarch, are printed in separate stanzas, answering to the four divisions.   By this arrangement, the eye at once detects the structure of the poem ; and the mind, relieved by the spaces, has more leisure to examine its beauties.   The sonnets in this volume are arranged after the

* *Encyclopædia Americana*, art. *Sonnet.*

Italian plan,—with the exception of uniting the two terzines, which appeared allowable since they are often closely connected in sense.

[2] Page 44. *America's Walhalla.*

Walhalla, or Valhalla—in the Scandinavian mythology, the paradise of heroes, after death. But it has been applied, in Germany, to a temple or edifice, in which are collected the names and statues of distinguished men.

[3] Page 45. *This ancient tree.*

The well known elm, which stands in the centre of the Common, usually called " the great tree."

[4] Page 48. *The Danish Tower at Newport.*

America was formerly thought to possess no " ruins," no relics of the past; but it appears that the "New World" is gradually turning out to be the older world of the two: so Sir Charles Lyle pronounces it,—geologically speaking, at least. But in addition to the remarkable monuments of the west and south, which go back beyond the memory of man,—the strange mounds scattered throughout the Mississippi Valley, and the extensive ruins found in Central America,—we have, in this tower at Newport, an interesting relic of the Middle Ages. It has been commonly called by the inhabitants " the old wind-mill," simply because no one knew what else to make of it. But Danish antiquarians pronounce it to have been the work of their ancestors,

L. of C.

the Northmen, who, it is now known, visited North America in the 11th or 12th century, at least 300 years before the time of Columbus. Professor Rafn, of Copenhagen, says of this tower: "Of the ancient structure in Newport, there are no ornaments remaining which might possibly have served to guide us in assigning the probable date of its erection. That no vestige whatever is found of the pointed arch, nor any approximation to it, is indicative of an earlier rather than a later period. From such characteristics as remain, however, we can scarcely form any other inference than one in which I am persuaded that all who are familiar with Old Northern architecture will concur,—that this building was erected at a period decidedly not later than the twelfth century. This remark applies, of course, to the original building only, and not to the alterations that it subsequently received. For there are several alterations in the upper part of the building, which cannot be mistaken, and which were most likely occasioned by its being adapted, in modern times, to various uses; for example, as the substructure of a windmill, and latterly, as a hay magazine. To the same times may be referred the windows, the fire-place, and the apertures made above the columns. That this building could not have been erected for a windmill, is what an architect will easily discern."

It is many years since I saw this structure; but it abides in my memory as a striking object—a round stone tower, some forty or fifty feet in height, resting upon eight columns. Had they this tower in England, how much they would make of it!

tastefully would they train over it the picturesque ivy, open vistas through which it could be seen to the best advantage, and preserve it with the utmost care.

⁵ Page 49.　*Ledyard, the Traveler.*

See Sparks's *Life of Ledyard.*

⁶ Page 50.　*Honor to Fulton and his native soil!*

Many attempts have been made to rob Fulton of his merit as the inventor of the steamboat. Others, no doubt, both in America and Europe, had conceived the idea before him, and some had even put it into partial execution; but it remained for Fulton, by a course of persevering and trying effort, to bring the invention into successful operation and use,—thus performing a great service to mankind. It has been wisely remarked, and the remark is strikingly applicable to the present case, "The world justly gives credit to the man who makes a discovery available, not to him who merely perceived it to be possible."* His first steamboat was launched upon the river Hudson, in the year 1807. Five years afterwards, namely, in 1812, Henry Bell succeeded in putting a steamboat into operation on the river Clyde, in Scotland. In sailing up that river, the traveler beholds, in a conspicuous position on its right bank, an obelisk, with the name and date inscribed upon it, "Henry Bell, 1812." Where is Fulton's monument?

* Lewes's *Life of Goethe.*

[7] **Page 51.** *The dead reviving at a touch, is seen ;*
—alluding to Allston's fine picture of the dead man reviving
on touching the bones of Elisha (2 Kings, xiii. 21.)

[8] Page 54.   See Lieut. Lynch's very interesting and well-
written narrative.

[9] **Page 55.**   *In search of England's lost ones ;*
—Sir John Franklin and his party,—the crews of the *Erebus*
and *Terror*,—who have, doubtless, long since perished amid the
polar snows.

[10] **Page 55.**   *No more, no more, those northern wilds to roam.*
Dr. Kane died at Havana, February 16, 1857, his constitution broken, doubtless, by the hardships endured in his polar
explorations.

[11] **Page 57.**   *The Father of waters.*
The *Mississippi,* which, in the Indian language, is said to
have this signification.

[12] Page 59.   *On moonlit groves was falling.*
On my last visit to Harvard, in 1857, I was pained to find
that pleasant grove of evergreens, which fronted old "Massachusetts," gone : the rude hands of "improvement" had laid
low, and left a bare lawn in its place.

THE END.